THE MAGIC CHRISTMAS PINECONE
A Bedtime Story

by E.L. Ferriter, Jr.

Illustrated by Emma J. Wright

For Mike and Regina, who always believed in the magic of fairy tales.

Can you keep a secret?

Then let me tell you a tale…

Once upon a time there was a quiet little boy named Eddie who was the youngest in a family of seven. They lived in a small town nestled in the rolling hills of New England where winter comes early and usually brings lots of snow.

He was a kind boy but life wasn't easy. You see, Eddie stood out. He had red curls, and bright blue eyes which made it easy for children to tease him. Because of this, he was very shy and had no friends.

While everybody, of course, loves snow, Eddie loved it more than anyone. He loved the dancing snowflakes. He loved the swirling mists. He loved to run through its perfect whiteness.

And his absolute favorite thing to do was to run into the early morning winter fog, where tiny ice crystals floated in the air like diamond dust.

Nobody knew that Eddie had a secret friend, hidden in the place where the mist was thickest. Who was this friend? Why, he was none other than the Great North Wind, and this is their story.

It all started on a cold winter's night. Eddie and his grandfather sat by the fire. Eddie's grandpa loved to tell stories about the Great North Wind.

"The Great North Wind is cruel," Eddie's grandpa said in a sharp, crackly, old-man voice that made all his words sound true.

"He has a heart of ice, and knows nothing of love."

"He is the death of many ships at sea..."

"...and the maker of fierce blizzards."

"Why, if the Great North Wind were here right now, he'd breathe his cold breath on you and turn you into a block of ice."

"Really?" Eddie gasped.

His grandpa nodded solemnly. "Really, and I know his real name. Hardly anybody knows that, but I do."

"What is it, Grandpa?" Eddie asked.

Eddie's grandpa looked first one way and then the other, as though he were making sure nobody else could hear.

He leaned forward and cupped his hand to the boy's ear.

"His name," the old man whispered, "is… Boreas."

Then he leaned back in his chair and gave Eddie a look, as if to say *don't ever tell anyone!*

Eddie thought about that. Was his grandpa making it up, or was it real? He wasn't sure. "Grandpa, can you tell me more about B-… I mean, the North Wind?"

If the North Wind really was cruel, maybe Eddie would have to re-think his love for winter. He hoped his grandpa was wrong.

"I think that's enough talk about the North Wind for tonight," he replied with a smile.

His grandfather walked him to bed, lovingly tucked him in and turned out the light.

But sleep didn't come easily that night. Eddie dreamed of fierce blizzards, and ships wrecks in icy graves. He pulled up the covers and curled into a tiny ball.

After a minute or two, he asked himself, "What am I so afraid of? It's just winter, and I love winter."

His grandpa couldn't be right. The North Wind was the kind friend who brought him snow to play in. How could anyone who makes the world so white and peaceful be described as cruel?

Eddie smiled, thinking of the beautiful snowy world outside, and fell softly to sleep.

The Magic Christmas Pine Cone

The next day, Eddie had an idea. He ran into the early morning fog, right into the middle of a great field where the mist was thickest. This was his secret place because the fog was filled with ice crystals.

He drew a deep breath and called at the top of his lungs:

"BO-RE-AS!"

There was no reply. Eddie waited a moment and tried again but the fog seemed to swallow up his voice.

"He must be somewhere else," Eddie thought. (After all, even the North Wind can't be everywhere at once.)

But he didn't know where else to look, and the cold fog was making his nose run.

He decided to go home and think about this some more. As he turned toward his house, he muttered, half to himself, "I just wanted you to know I believe you're good."

S uddenly, the fog began to shift and change...

First it billowed around Eddie's feet, then climbed up and formed a huge face in the mist behind him. Eddie felt as if someone was watching, so he turned. In shock, he stood motionless as a giant face looked down upon him.

The face looked like a wise old man, with waves of mist drifting behind him forming his long white hair. He had a thick white beard, too. The mist-man filled the sky. Eddie felt very, very tiny in front of him.

Eddie's heart went *BANG BANG BANG* in his chest as he saw the giant face stare at him.

The Magic Christmas Pine Cone

Nobody moved for a moment. Eddie heard something he thought must be thunder, until he noticed the giant face was taking a deep breath.

It sucked in the fog all around him like a huge vacuum. The North Wind paused for just a moment, and then the giant beard parted again…

"Here it comes," thought Eddie.

His grandpa had been right, and the next thing he would feel would be the icy breath of the North Wind turning him into a block of ice forever.

He didn't want to be a block of ice! He closed his eyes and braced himself for the deadly blast.

The Magic Christmas Pine Cone

However, something else happened.

Eddie heard a soft chiming sound and felt a frosty mist cover him. When he opened his eyes and looked down, he saw that his whole body was covered with sparkly purple frost.

Eddie was relieved he had not been turned into a block of ice. But there was something else, he didn't feel cold. Not even a little.

He looked up at Boreas in surprise.

The Magic Christmas Pine Cone

Boreas spoke. *"It's been a very long time since anyone has called to me, let alone a child,"* he said in a deep, foggy voice.

"My grandpa says you're cruel and bad," said Eddie.

"Not exactly," Boreas replied.

"Are you good, then?" asked Eddie.

"No, not that either. I just…"

There was a pause.

"You're just what?" asked Eddie.

"I just… am," replied Boreas.

Eddie thought about that. "Is your heart really made of ice?"

"Of course," Boreas said, smiling. *"What else would it be made of?"*

Eddie supposed that was true. "But, do you really tip over ships and make blizzards?"

"Sometimes," Boreas admitted. *"But I also give the trees and flowers a long, cool rest, so they can turn green after I'm gone. and I make snow for little boys and girls to play in."*

"So that's what you mean when you say you just… are," said Eddie.

Boreas smiled hugely in his big frosty beard, glad to find someone who understood and loved him.

"Little boy, I'm going to give you a present."

"Every Christmas, you'll wake up in the morning and look out your window to see that I've left you a beautiful blanket of snow."

Eddie couldn't imagine anything better.

Eddie and Boreas met often after that. Boreas enjoyed their friendship and many times he would shape the fog into beautiful scenes showing the places around the world where he went. They learned a lot from each other and became close friends.

One day, Eddie thought of something he'd never thought to ask before. "Boreas, is Santa real?"

"*Yes,*" smiled the North Wind. "*St. Nicholas does exist. I gave him a present, too.*"

"Like mine?" asked Eddie.

"*I gave him something else. I made him immortal, so he can go on bringing presents to children forever. I also gave him a spell so his home is hidden and nobody can ever disturb him.*"

The fog swirled. Instead of the big bearded face of his friend, Eddie saw a beautiful village with a castle as its crowning jewel.

The Magic Christmas Pine Cone

The fog shifted again and he saw a high wall of ice with a giant totem pole at one end.

"This is the magic gate." said Boreas.

"Someday I hope you will go there. To open it, you must stand before the gate, take a handful of snow, throw it into the air and say the magic word."

"What is it?" asked Eddie.

"The magic word is an ancient name for the South Wind, but first you must promise me that you will keep that name a secret, as you do mine."

"I promise," said Eddie.

"The South Wind's name is Moriah."

Eddie thought that was the most beautiful name he'd ever heard. He thanked Boreas for trusting him, and never doubted the existence of Santa again.

The Magic Christmas Pine Cone

On the following day, Eddie asked, "what's your home like? Where do you live?"

"I live in an ice cave at the top of the highest mountain, near the North Pole, far too high and too cold for any human to reach," Boreas replied.

Boreas used his trick of shaping the fog to show Eddie his home.

"Don't you get lonely?" asked Eddie.

"Sometimes."

Boreas looked sad for a moment. *"But coming here makes me feel better."*

Eddie was glad to hear that.

"One other thing makes me feel better," said Boreas.

With his breath, he made a little flurry of wind and snow. Eddie saw something round and brown that Boreas's breath blew up into the air, and he caught it in his mittened hands. It was a pinecone.

"A pinecone makes you feel better?" he asked.

How could a tiny pinecone make the North Wind feel anything?

"The rest of the world hides away when the North Wind comes to call," said Boreas. *"Only the pine tree greets me with life and happiness."*

"And me," Eddie pointed out. "I do, too."

For a moment, Boreas looked a little startled. Then he laughed.

"And you too, Eddie."

The Magic Christmas Pine Cone

Years passed, and Eddie grew. His shoulders became broad and strong. All the while, he kept the pinecone in the top drawer of his nightstand.

The year he turned eighteen, Eddie went out to greet Boreas as always but something was different and Boreas could feel it.

"Boreas," Eddie said.

"I wanted to thank you for your friendship. I'm not afraid of the world anymore. I want to see all the wonderful places you showed me."

He paused for a moment then he said. "I'm here to say goodbye... at least for now."

He paused again. "Don't worry, I'll be back."

Boreas had known this day might come. Boys become men and lose the magic of their childhood. Boreas's face turned sad. Eddie turned and slowly walked away. As he disappeared into the fog, Boreas called out to him.

"Remember me."

His voice echoed, and then it faded into silence. The fog that made Boreas's face began to blur and drift. As it returned to mist, a single icy tear fell to the snow.

Time passed and the North Wind saw no further need to keep the promise he made to the boy. Snow arrived less often to the small town in time for the holidays.

After a while, all they received were cold windy nights with an ice storm or two.

Eddie was a grown-up now, doing grown-up things.
But even grown-ups remember their childhood and its secrets.

Many years passed and Eddie felt the need to return home. Christmas was coming and it was his turn to share fire side stories. On Christmas Eve, Eddie gathered his nieces and nephews to the fireside. He spun many stories about the wonderful places he'd been. The children were full of questions, but it was getting late and it was time to go to bed.

"Off you go then," Eddie said.

The children slowly started to go. All but one. It was Andrew, who stayed in his chair, looking stubborn.

"Is something wrong, Andrew?" asked Eddie.

Andrew waited, and then blurted, "Is Santa real, Uncle Eddie?"

All the children sat back down to hear their uncle's answer.

Eddie didn't hesitate. "Of course he is! I've seen his home. The North Wind showed it to me."

"The North Wind?" all the children shouted.

"Yes," Eddie said. "He's my friend."

Nobody was going to go to bed after hearing that – so, even though it was getting late, Eddie shared the story of his friendship with the North Wind.

He told the children everything he knew about Santa's home, and the secret gate made from a great wall of ice. He even got out the pinecone Boreas had given him and let them touch it.

But he kept his promise and did not tell them the South Wind's secret name.

By the time he was finished, it was so late, the fire was a pile of glowing embers.

"Okay, everybody, it's bedtime," Eddie announced and began shooing all the children up the stairs.

But when he turned, Andrew was still sitting there. "Why don't we get snow for Christmas anymore?" he asked.

"No snow?" Eddie was surprised.

"None for a long time," Andrew said gloomily. "Think you could ask your friend the North Wind to bring it back?"

"I'll take care of it first thing in the morning," Eddie replied with a smile, and shooed him off to bed.

Christmas dawned clear and snowless, but Boreas was nowhere to be found. This puzzled Eddie at first, but then he remembered: Boreas only came when there was fog to help him take form. Nevertheless, Santa had come and all the children were happily opening their gifts.

Later that morning, when the hubbub had died down, Andrew asked, "So, what about my snow?"

"No fog," Eddie shrugged. "Boreas can't come when the sky is bright."

"Yeah, right," said Andrew, looking away.

Eddie sighed at the sight of his nephew's sadness. "C'mon, let's talk."

The two sat down together on the stairs.

"It is too late for me to do anything this year, but I promise – by next Christmas, I'll bring snow."

Andrew smiled in spite of himself. "Really? Cross your heart?"

Eddie crossed his heart and looked over Andrew's shoulder.

"Now don't you think you've been away from your presents a bit too long?"

"Presents!" Andrew gasped, and dashed away.

A few minutes later, he heard,

"Dinnertime!"

...and the house exploded with noise, as dozens of feet rushed toward the rich smells coming from the kitchen.

Eddie just sat there and thought. How was he going to fulfill his promise?

"Well, I guess there's only one thing to do," he said to himself.

After a moment, he stood up and went to join the others for dinner.

A nd so it was that Eddie began his journey to the North Pole.

With the help of some friends he had made in his travels, Eddie slowly worked his way north.

He endured many hardships along the way, but he eventually reached the last leg of his journey.

As he moved steadily along on a dog sled, his goal was finally in sight.

However, disaster was close at hand…

The air suddenly became still. There was something else, something coming from behind. He stopped the sled and looked back.

His eyes got as wide as dinner plates when he saw a towering wall of snow bearing down on him. It stretched from one horizon to the other and went as high as the eye could see. It moved at him like a giant rolling wave.

He madly rushed the dogs ahead but it was too late. The blizzard crashed down upon him with the force of an avalanche.

Everything was a white-out. Eddie couldn't hear anything over the roar of the storm.

The sled ran over an outcrop in the ice and heaved into the air. Eddie was caught by surprise, lost his grip and fell off.

He wandered through the blizzard for a long time. Eventually he found an ice shelf to hide under and waited for the storm to end. Hours passed and he slowly fell asleep.

When he woke, it was eerily quiet. He walked out into a clear star lit night to see he'd arrived at the giant wall of ice. It was just as Boreas had shown him so long ago.

The snow sparkled on the ground like tiny diamonds as far as the eye could see.

He watched his breath freeze in the air as he said, "I made it."

He took a step closer and looked up at the huge wall which loomed before him.

He took a deep breath then gently reached down and gathered a handful of snow. It sparkled in his hand. Eddie threw it high into the air and yelled the magic word of enchantment as loud as he could.

"Moriah!"

He heard it echo off the canyon walls then softly fade away. Everything fell silent and the snow softly fell to the ground.

Nothing happened…

But eventually, something did.

Across the great void he heard the soft sound of a woman's voice lightly singing on the air. Then a gentle breeze came drifting across the snow around his feet.

Eddie was motionless as he heard the light tinkling of wind chimes as the wind blew the shimmering snowflakes that lay all around his boots up the great wall of ice.

Suddenly, the Northern Lights flashed across the sky in a rainbow of colors. The light caught in the snow as it sparkled in the air. Within moments, the magic gate appeared as glowing lines in the ice.

In the magical lines he saw beautiful designs of all shapes and sizes. It was the most amazing thing he had ever seen.

That was until he saw Moriah.

She appeared in a swirling vortex of snow with white flowing hair and a shimmering silver gown that gently moved in the air around her.

Eddie was stunned by her beauty. She simply smiled back at him standing in the snow.

He watched as she lightly waived her arms before the gate. The glowing lines parted and the ice gave a great crackling pop as the giant gate began to open. Mist flowed out, as the doors came to rest.

Eddie thanked Moriah and stepped inside.

Upon arriving in the valley on the other side, he found the village was just as the North Wind had shown him so many years before. The elves came to greet him with warm smiles, accompanied by his very happy sled dogs, their tails wagging.

The Magic Christmas Pine Cone

In no time at all they escorted Eddie to Santa's castle and Santa gladly agreed to take Eddie to the cave of the North Wind. Santa stayed in the sleigh as Eddie went in. Eddie felt very small as he walked inside the enormous cave.

An eerie blue glow shone through small cracks in the walls. The air was so full of mist and ice crystals that it was very hard to see. Eddie began to worry.

"What if Boreas doesn't remember me?" he thought.

Suddenly, he was almost blown off his feet by a huge blast of wind.

"WHO DARES ENTER MY CAVE?"

The rumbling voice was so deep that it felt like it was shaking his very bones.

Eddie faltered. "It… It… It's me. Eddie. You knew me when I was a boy. I've come back now, as a man."

The familiar face formed out of the fog, huge and stern.

The Magic Christmas Pine Cone

"How can this be? I thought you had forgotten me, as all children do."

"How could I forget you? You're my friend!" Eddie pointed out, held out his hand and showed Boreas the pinecone.

"I have a gift, for you."

"Remember? You told me once, that you admired these. You said that pine trees were the only thing that greeted you with life and happiness."

Boreas's foggy eyebrows rose and he looked into Eddie's bright blue eyes.

"I remember, young Eddie," the North Wind rumbled, *"the pine trees, and you."*

"I just went away for a while," Eddie explained. "I went to see all the wonderful places you showed me as a child."

He paused. "I never thought this would be one of them," he finished with a smirk.

Boreas's mighty laugh shook the walls. Eddie grinned at sight of his friend, happy again.

The two began to talk.

The Magic Christmas Pine Cone

He told Boreas about his travels and the promise he made to Andrew. The North Wind thought for a moment.

Finally, he said, *"place your gift on the floor and step back."*

Eddie watched, Boreas pursed his great lips and blew a whispering breath that sounded like the tinkle of falling icicles. The pinecone suddenly glistened with a fine coating of ice crystals that made it shimmer in the pale blue light.

"This cone is now enchanted," the North Wind explained. *"If you place it on a windowsill, it will summon the winter snows.*

"But the boy must promise to take it down by the end of winter, for all seasons need their turn in the cycle of life."

"I promise, and thank you," said Eddie.

He bid his friend farewell and started his journey home.

The Magic Christmas Pine Cone

Once again, the children gathered by the fire with their beloved uncle. This time he told them of his greatest adventure: visiting the North Wind's home. After he had finished, he gave Andrew the magical pinecone. Andrew held it up for all of the children to see. Its frosty edges sparkled in the fire light. Andrew eagerly promised to do as the North Wind had asked.

Later that night, Eddie found the boy fast asleep, the magic pinecone lovingly placed on the sill by his bed.

Looking through the frosty glass, he watched snow softly falling.

To this day, pinecones are given on Christmas Eve as gifts of love and friendship, reminding us to keep love in our hearts, so magic will always be with us.

THE END

ACKNOWLEDGEMENTS

I would like to take a moment to show my sincere gratitude to the following children's literary organizations, foundations and people who made this book possible. I always find myself in a state of awe when I witness such wonderful acts of kindness. These folks perform miracles every day and I'd like to shine a light on them as a token of my respect and admiration.

First and foremost, I'd like to thank my very talented artist and illustrator,
Emma J Wright.
Her imagination was inspiring and she always surprised me with new ideas.
She's always a joy to work.
http://paintedlyrics.com
Instagram: @emjsart
Emma resides in Australia.

Book Donation Programs:
Lisa's Libraries: lisalibraries.org
First Book: firstbook.org
Read to Grow: readtogrow.org

Children's Literacy Programs:
Supporting member of the following:
NAEYC: naeyc.org
Jumpstart: jstart.org
NHSA: nhsa.org
Reading Is Fundamental: rif.org
SCBWI: scbwi.org

Foundations:
Endeavor Foundation for the Arts
San Francisco, CA.
https://nonprofitlocator.org/organizations/ca/san-francisco/452455967-endeavor-foundation-for-the-art
The Literacy Empowerment Foundation: lefbooks.org